My Pet Turtle

by Deborah Reber
illustrated by David Cutting

Ready-to-Read

Simon Spotlight / Nick Jr.

New York   London   Toronto   Sydney   Singapore

To my wonderful dog and forever puppy, Ari.—D. R.

For my Uncle, Henry Seegitz, whose influence
I could not have done without.—D. C.

NOTE TO PARENTS:
Welcome to the series of Ready-to-Read books done the
Blue's Clues way! This line of books has been researched for
preschoolers to ensure a high level of interactivity in this
simple rebus format. Preschoolers are encouraged to read
along with you by identifying the pictures above the words in
this story. Because the word is also underneath each picture,
your preschooler will begin to recognize each word as well!
What's more, this line of books is written from Blue's
preschooler point of view and reveals her feelings
about the world around her.

Based on the TV series *Blue's Clues*® created by Traci Paige Johnson,
Todd Kessler, and Angela C. Santomero as seen on Nick Jr.®
On *Blue's Clues*, Steve is played by Steven Burns.

SIMON SPOTLIGHT
An imprint of Simon & Schuster Children's Publishing Division
1230 Avenue of the Americas, New York, New York 10020
Manufactured in The United States of America
First Edition   2 4 6 8 10 9 7 5 3 1
ISBN 0-689-84186-8
Library of Congress Catalog Card Number 00-109544

Hello! I am .
BLUE
Have you met my
pet , Turquoise?
TURTLE

Turquoise was a birthday from Steve.

PRESENT

He gave me the
PRESENT
after I blew out the
on my .
CANDLES   CAKE

Inside the 🎁 (PRESENT) was my 🐢 (TURTLE), Turquoise! She smiled at me. I knew we would be friends!

My 🐢, Turquoise,
TURTLE
lives in my bedroom.

She stays on the TABLE
next to my  BED.

My 🐢, Turquoise
TURTLE
lives in a glass 📦.
TANK

She has sand and
a rock in her .

TANK

I take care of my 🐢,
TURTLE
Turquoise, by feeding
her every morning.

She likes to eat ,

, and .

My  , Turquoise,
TURTLE
needs to drink.
WATER

Every day I put fresh  in her .

WATER

BOWL

One day we had
show-and-tell at .

SCHOOL

I brought my  in a
TURTLE
glass to show my
BOWL
friends!

Turquoise sat on my desk in her glass !

BOWL

She liked SCHOOL very much.

Sometimes my 🐢,
TURTLE
Turquoise, sits with
me on the 🌿.
GRASS
She loves the ☀️.
SUN
It makes her happy.

When it is time to go to 🛏 BED we read a 📖 BOOK together.

Turquoise loves to read with me.

I love my 🐢,
TURTLE
Turquoise! She is
a great pet and
a very good friend.